TREE THE TRUNK AND THE TUBA

JANET STOTT-THORNTON
Illustrated by Chris Lynch

For Alan and Nick, who both play tuba

Written by Janet Stott-Thornton
Illustrated by Chris Lynch
Designed by Peter Shaw

Published by Mimosa Publications Pty Ltd
PO Box 779, Hawthorn 3122, Australia
© 1995 Mimosa Publications Pty Ltd

Literacy 2000 is a Trademark registered in the
United States Patent and Trademark Office.

Distributed in the United States of America by

Rigby
A Division of Reed Elsevier Inc.
500 Coventry Lane
Crystal Lake, IL 60014
800-822-8661

Distributed in Canada by
PRENTICE HALL GINN
1870 Birchmount Road
Scarborough
Ontario M1P 2J7

99 98
10 9 8 7 6 5 4 3
Printed in Hong Kong through Bookbuilders Ltd

ISBN 0 7327 1572 5

CONTENTS

ONE

The Trunk and the Tree

Everything began the day Cilla went nuts in the hall. Cilla's my cat. Before that, I hadn't even noticed the old chest hidden in the shadows of the front hallway among all our moving crates and cartons. I'd been thinking about more important things – like why we had to come to live in this boring town anyway. Nobody understood the way I felt.

"Please stop complaining, Sophie. How do you know it's boring when you've only been here a week?" That was all the sympathy I got from Dad.

"Moving to a new place can be exciting, dear. Just give it a chance!" And that was Mom. See? Not a speck of understanding!

I suppose I should go right back to the beginning and explain why we moved. One day a letter arrived, telling us that some old relative named Mrs. Leach had died and left us this house. Tom and I had never even heard of her until then.

"Family conference," Dad announced that evening. "In the dining room, now!"

I put up a fight about moving, but I could tell that everyone else wanted to go, so I didn't have much choice.

So we moved to this town where we didn't know anyone. Mom and Dad were thrilled, because it would be cheaper to live here. Tom thought it was cool, because we were just down the street from a sports center with a basketball court.

But as far as I was concerned, it was the worst thing that had ever happened to me. I'd had to leave all my friends behind at my old school. (They promised to write every week – but I'll believe that when I see it!)

I was so miserable that when I first saw the house I nearly burst into tears. It gave me the creeps the way it crouched half-hidden in the big overgrown yard. I remember wondering out loud about the old lady who had lived here.

"What kind of person would want to live in a place like this? I'm just glad we never knew her – I would have hated coming here for vacation."

"Look, Sofa," (Tom always calls me Sofa) "Dad said she was nearly a hundred. What were you expecting – an ultra-modern apartment crammed with technology?"

"So how was she related to us, anyway? A great-aunt?"

"Get real! More like a great-great-aunt, at that age."

I threw a pillow at him.

But apart from her age we didn't know anything about her. We didn't really know any other relatives, either – they lived too far away and, from all accounts, they weren't very exciting anyway.

So this was the way things were the day Cilla went crazy. She'd been hiding behind the long red velvet curtains, leaping out and pouncing on my feet as I walked past. Then she suddenly leaped across to the chest in the corner of the hallway and slid along the top, hooking the lace cloth in her claws and knocking an old vase full of faded paper flowers to the floor. Dust flew into the air in all directions, making us both sneeze.

Cilla looked so surprised that I laughed. Cats don't like being laughed at, especially Cilla. She turned her back on me and stalked away up the stairs. I went after her and tried to grab her, but she was too slippery. Tom was on his way downstairs, bouncing his basketball.

"What's wrong with Cilla? He-*ey*, will you look at this!"

He dragged me over to the old chest, and pointed at all the labels and stickers on it from different towns and countries. It was made of leather, and had metal corners and clasps.

"Maybe it's full of rare jewels and we're on the verge of making our fortune," I said sarcastically.

It wasn't locked. Tom opened the lid and peered in. The smell of mothballs wafted out as he lifted up some tissue paper. He took out something black and flat and round. It popped out suddenly, and I jumped a mile! It was an old-fashioned top hat, the kind men wear in black-and-white movies on TV.

Tom put it on. "Cool, huh?"

I tried not to laugh, but I was beginning to feel interested. Tom took out another layer of tissue paper. Under it was a heavy

black coat with long tails, lined with silk. I helped him lift it out.

"I wonder whose stuff this is. Looks like our mysterious great-great-aunt was an ancient magician or something!"

This I liked. "Imagine it! Or maybe her husband was, and she used to creak her way out of his magic box when he zapped it with his wand!"

Tom threw out more tissue paper, and this time found a mask that covered just the top half of his face when he put it on. It looked pretty weird with the hat.

"It suits you!" I said, meaning it didn't. "Let me look."

After all, I'd discovered the chest in the first place – or rather, Cilla had – and I was still hoping for jewelry or money. That might mean we could afford to move back to our old place.

"There's something really big down at the bottom." As soon as I saw it I knew it was some kind of musical instrument, but I didn't know what – it had a big mouth, and coiled metal tubes. I think I must have gasped, because Dad came into the hall to see what the noise was about.

"It's a tuba," Dad said in a puzzled way. "What's it doing in there? What a beauty!"

(What a *disappointment*, I thought.)

He lifted it out and inspected it closely. "Well, it's quite a find, and just look at all this stuff!"

"It was all in this old chest," I said.

"Actually, it's a traveling trunk," said Dad helpfully. "Look at all the stickers. These old things obviously belonged to a person who moved around a lot."

Then Tom started playing detective. "Any clues in the pockets?" He checked the coat, and pulled out a white bow tie. "Look,

it's got something written on the back – "SS." What could that mean, Dad?"

Dad scratched his head. "Well, it could be a secret code, but it's more likely to be someone's initials."

"Or the organization they worked for," drawled Tom. "The Secret Service, I mean. This is obviously an elaborate disguise, and the person who wore it was a spy."

"So, Detective Florimell, what's it doing in an old lady's hallway? Just answer that!" I said.

"The best spies are always the people you'd least suspect. It seems to me that our great-great-aunt only *appeared* to be a harmless old lady living alone in a big, ramshackle house. And I suggest we dig a little deeper into this trunk of hers for further clues..."

At this, we threw out all the paper in the trunk and looked in every pocket of the coat and in the lining of the top hat, but we didn't find anything else. Then Tom, tired of playing detective, wandered off – probably to practice slamdunking again at the basketball ring Dad had put up on the garage wall.

Dad helped me repack the trunk. When I was halfway up the stairs I went back to get the hat. I liked the way it popped out, then folded down flat again.

"I bet that stupid Georgina doesn't have anything like this!"

I haven't told you about Georgina yet – not that you've missed much. You see, I wasn't enjoying my new school, either. For one thing, there was the class project to worry about; and for another, Georgina and her friends Amanda and Jacinta, the two copycats, seemed to think that new kids were there to be bullied. In fact, I'd only been at school a couple of days when Georgina grabbed my arm while the teacher was writing on the board and pinched me really hard. And the next day she stepped on my lunch.

On top of that, Ms. Parkinson, our teacher, had assigned the worst possible project: "My Family Tree." Luckily, she said I didn't have to do as much as the others, as the class had already been working on it for a while. I was secretly glad to hear that I only had to choose one branch of my family, but Georgina, who had traced her family tree back about two hundred years, wasn't at all impressed with that. "Your family's probably so boring that you'd put us to sleep telling us about even half of it," she'd said, "so it's just as well you've been let off the hook."

Still, Georgina was really only part of my problem, and in a way, she was right. The one branch of my family I knew about, besides Mom, Dad, and Tom, of course, was hardly interesting. Instead of a branch, it was more like a pathetic twig.

I was going to ask Dad what I could do, but he was still worrying about where he'd packed the bathroom scale or last year's plum jelly. (He's always making jelly.) And Mom must have been busy with a writing job of her own, because the first thing she'd unpacked was her computer.

But after Cilla discovered the trunk I had an idea. I'd *invent* a really amazing branch for my family tree. Mom was always saying I had a good imagination, so why not use it? No one at school would know the difference. Of course, I hadn't counted on Georgina and her friends – but I'll tell you about that later.

Before supper, I looked around the house in dark corners and musty closets to see

if any other interesting things had been hidden away – maybe family heirlooms, or some pictures painted by famous people; but all I found were some dusty rolled-up rugs and a chipped cup.

So that night I drew up the unusual theatrical branch of my family tree. "This ought to shut that Georgina up," I thought, as I invented my fantastic new relatives.

TWO

The Trick

The next day, I took the project to school. It included Great-uncle René, who had worn the white tie and tails and played the tuba, and Uncle Marmaduke (Duke for short), who had been a magician and owned the top hat. (I'd decided, just to play it safe, that they'd both died some years ago.) There was also a second cousin, who worked in a traveling carnival with Madame Mystery the Fortune Teller.

Ms. Parkinson was extremely impressed. Georgina wasn't. She glared at me, and I could tell that lunch hour wasn't going to be much fun.

As soon as the bell rang, Georgina and company went off to their favorite corner

21

of the playground for a meeting. I ate my lunch quickly, so it couldn't be stepped on. "Unless they step on me!" I thought. I decided the library was a good place to go, but somehow they found me there.

Georgina pinched my arm. "We don't believe your relatives were really all that amazing – do we?" She looked at Amanda and Jacinta.

They shook their heads in unison, reminding me of those open-mouthed clowns at sideshows.

"We think you're just making it all up, don't we?"

The clowns nodded.

"We don't like liars, do we?"

This time they shuffled their feet, their clown faces drooping as they slowly wagged their heads.

"Well, I can show you their things – in the big trunk at home," I said quickly.

"What makes you think we want to come to your creepy old place? Looks like a haunted house!"

"Are you too scared?"

"We're not scared of anything – are we, girls? 'Specially not you and your oddball relatives!"

"My oddball relatives, as you call them, are not likely to be there, because they're dead. At least I don't *think* they'll be at home." I said the last bit to myself, because I'd just had another idea. I wondered if Tom would mind helping me out. "All right," I continued, "you can come over tomorrow after school."

That night I told Mom and Dad about my project, in case anyone said the wrong thing the next afternoon. (I didn't tell them about my new idea, though – not yet, anyway.)

Dad wasn't really happy that I'd been making up stories, and said I ought to think about that. He wasn't too mad, though, because after our discovery he supposed they might be partly true. Mom just smiled and said, "There, I always knew you took after me," and went back to her computer.

When I told Tom my idea, he readily agreed to help me. "I've seen that Georgina and her gang at school. Her brother's in my class; he's just as rotten. It must run in the family."

So we had a meeting that night to plan the surprise. Tom said he would run home after school the next day, and I agreed to

try to take longer than usual, just to make sure he would arrive well before us.

As it turned out, I had to take even more bullying for my trouble, because Georgina started calling me a snail.

"We don't have all day – do we, girls? Anyone would think she'd just made up all that stuff about her family and had absolutely nothing to show us!"

They agreed as usual. Amanda and Jacinta were as spineless as jellyfish, and Georgina was just a big, bullying shark. But this time, I thought, I can afford to ignore them.

When we reached our house, I opened the front door into the gloomy hallway.

"Is it always this dark at your place?" sneered Georgina.

I didn't even answer her – I was too busy hoping that Tom had been able to get ready in time. But just then I heard the weirdest noises coming from behind the long red curtains at the end of the hall – like nothing I'd ever heard before. Amanda and Jacinta began looking at each other nervously, but the strange sounds didn't seem to bother Georgina.

"Is someone standing on your cat's tail, Silly Sophie?"

"My cat doesn't make noises like that," I whispered. "I don't know what it is!"

Just then the curtains opened and a strange figure appeared. It was difficult to see because the light was coming from behind it. It was wearing a tall hat and old-fashioned clothes, and a mask that covered the top half of its face. The noises were coming from the large instrument it carried as it advanced toward us down the long hallway.

I screamed a long piercing scream and backed toward the front door. "It's come

back!" I shouted. "Run!" And as I ran down the path through the tangled yard to the gate, I risked a glance behind me. Sure enough, all three girls were right behind me. Even Georgina was racing along like a terrified rabbit with a hunter on its tail. But when we reached the gate, her fear turned to anger. "You'll pay for this!" she snarled, as she stormed off with Amanda and Jacinta sniveling behind her.

Tom and I didn't stop laughing for hours afterward. It made eating difficult. Mom was working on a new story outline at the table and was only mildly annoyed at our giggling, but Dad was more concerned.

"I hope you haven't been up to anything you shouldn't," he sighed. "I saw those girls running out the gate as if something horrible was after them."

"It was!" we announced together, and started laughing again.

Dad decided we should wash and dry the dishes, as a sort of punishment, but we didn't mind.

"That was a great sound you made on the tuba," I told Tom in admiration.

"Not knowing how to play it helped," he said, plunging his hands into the soapy water. "Tubas don't sound anything like that usually. Remember Tubby the Tuba?"

"He wasn't scary. Not like the Monstrous Masked Musician that was haunting this place this afternoon!"

Tom flicked some suds at me, and we ended up having a water fight. At that, Dad sent us off to bed.

THREE

The Old Theater

The next afternoon, I went to the back of the yard and climbed my Thinking Tree. If a "family tree" was real, I thought, it would look like this – a big broad trunk, solid as a rock, with a network of roots anchoring it to the ground. My Thinking Tree also has a comfortable place where the trunk forks into branches, just right for sitting and pondering the world.

But on this afternoon, my thoughts kept floating off like bunches of balloons. Even though I had managed to get away with faking my family tree and scaring Georgina and company, things still didn't feel right. Now, if anything, I felt even more bored than before. I wished my family tree really

was interesting. I wished that Georgina
wouldn't bully me. I wished ... Then Cilla
ran up the trunk as if something was after
her, and leaped on to a branch beside me.

"Who's a clever girl?" I stroked her fur
as she settled into what I call her sphinx
position. She stared out over the streets
and gardens, slowly swinging her tail. Cats

and dogs sometimes do that – they look at a spot in the air until they've got you looking at it, too. Usually there's nothing there. But this time, when I followed Cilla's gaze, I saw something that I hadn't noticed before.

It was quite a few streets away, at the end of a row of stores, not on the way to school at all. It seemed to be the shell of a big building, far larger than anything else in the area. I wondered what it was.

Cilla beat me by miles as we raced down the tree. She darted across the lawn and disappeared into the house. I found her waiting by the front door, looking up at me hopefully. Sometimes I think Cilla can read my mind, and this time she was certainly right – I'd decided to take her for a walk. People think she's unusual because she enjoys being taken out on a leash, but some Burmese cats are like that.

"Just taking Cilla for a walk, Mom!" I yelled, and was just about to escape as she materialized at the study door.

"Get some milk, will you, honey? The money's in the jar. Jar, far, bar...bees, knees, freeze..." and she disappeared again.

"Mom must be writing poetry now," I told Cilla as we hurried along the sidewalk, "or a rock song!" My cat seemed to know exactly where we were going.

Even though it had looked a long way away, the ruined building loomed around a corner much sooner than I expected. As we got closer I could see it hadn't been an office block, or stores, but some sort of old...

"Theater," said a voice behind me. "It was an old theater."

I jumped around in fright, tangling Cilla's leash with my legs and nearly falling over. An old woman, hardly taller than myself, leaned out of a gap in the fence.

"Sorry, Miss – didn't mean to startle you."
She came out onto the sidewalk and patted
Cilla, who immediately began purring
around her legs. "Lovely creatures, cats."

"Who are you?" I asked, hoping it didn't
sound too rude. She didn't seem to mind.

"My name's Alice," she said brightly. "I
live next door, above the store. I've known
this old place for a long time – since long
before the fire. My brother used to be the
theater caretaker, and we still keep an eye
on things. Sometimes I just like to go in
and remember it the way it used to be."

Looking through the fence, I could see
the blackened bricks and peeling paint.
"What happened?"

"No one really knows. It hadn't been used
as a theater for a long time. One night last
year it caught fire. The city officials are
still arguing about what to do with it. It's a
great pity."

She shook her head, smiling gently. "But
we saved some things before then. Would
you like to see them?"

I nodded and she led the way to the store
next door. A bell above the door rang as we
entered, and an old man popped up from
behind the wooden counter. His white hair
reminded me of dandelion fluff.

"My brother, Harry – the caretaker," said
Alice.

"Hello – I'm Sophie. And this is Cilla!"

"Hello," said Harry kindly. "I'll be with
you both in just a moment." And with that,
the caretaker disappeared again.

I looked around the dimly lit store. It was hard to say what it sold, exactly – there were shelves of things that looked interesting, but I couldn't tell what they were. I was just going to examine them more closely when the caretaker came back with a tray of cookies and juice, and a saucer of milk for Cilla.

Seeing this, Cilla jumped down from a tattered pile of rolled-up cylinders, knocking them with her leash. They fell, cascading to the floor.

"I'm sorry about that," I said, bending down to pick them up.

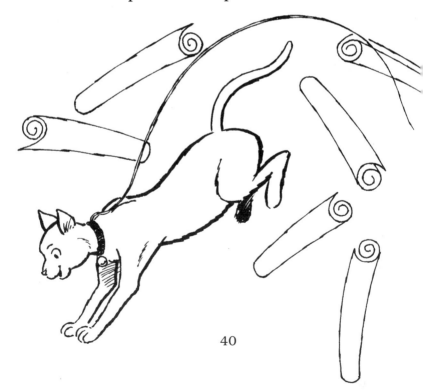

"That's all right – just a lot of old posters from the theater. Have a look if you want," said the caretaker.

The posters seemed very old – nearly as old as Harry and Alice. I wondered if my great-great-aunt had visited the theater next door. I began to unroll one of the dusty black and white posters. The one I'd picked looked like an advertising poster for a dance or a band or something. I began unrolling it further to have a closer look, but then I realized that something was bothering me. But I couldn't think what exactly was wrong, except maybe that it was getting late, and Mom would probably be wondering where I was.

"Look, I'm sorry, but I should be getting back. It's been really nice meeting you!"

"You'll come and see us again?"

"Yes, I will," I said, "and thank you. Come on, Cilla." Then I knew what the problem was. I couldn't see Cilla anywhere.

But no sooner had I thought this than I heard an awful wailing sound – worse than the noise Tom had made with the tuba. Only this time it was Cilla! It was her "alarm" voice...

FOUR

Top Hat and Tails

"It's coming from next door." Alice and the caretaker were out the door and into the street even before me. "I think someone must be in there. You stay here," said the caretaker as he climbed through the fence.

"Cilla's my cat. She might be hurt," I said, following him in. "I'm coming with you."

The wailing was now sounding closer and more urgent. We worked our way through a tumble of charred leather seats to the stage. Cilla came running up to me out of the dark, trailing her leash.

I picked her up. "There's a good kitty. What is it?"

Then I jumped with fright as a sound came from somewhere toward the back of the stage. "Help! Help me out of here!"

43

I walked carefully over to a shadowy heap on the floor. "Georgina! What are you doing here?"

"I... er... I followed your cat in here. I was worried about it when I saw it coming into this place."

Yeah Georgina, sure you were, I thought to myself, wondering just what she'd really been planning to do with my cat.

The caretaker seemed to be having some doubts about Georgina's story as well. "Are you sure about that now?" he asked her. "Lucky for you the boards are only burned in places." Georgina, obviously embarrassed, kept her eyes on the floor. We grabbed an arm each and hauled Georgina up. Her ankle was scratched and scraped, and one of her shoes had fallen under the stage.

"Too bad!" I said, with a little satisfaction. "No one's going under there for your smelly old shoe. Let's get out of here."

She looked so ridiculous hobbling along on one-and-a-half feet that I began to feel sorry for her. "I suppose you'd better come to my place and borrow a pair of my shoes," I sighed. "Your house is miles away."

"Don't do me any favors," she muttered. But after I'd thanked Harry and Alice and promised to visit them again, Georgina came with me.

From the end of our driveway I could see Tom practicing at the basketball ring. When he saw Georgina with me, his mouth dropped open in amazement.

"Mom's been wondering where you were," he said. "You were supposed to be getting some milk."

"Suffering succotash! I forgot about it."

"It's okay – I'll go, Sofa," he said.

I could see that Tom was curious about why Georgina was at our place, minus a shoe, but he's one of the good guys and so didn't say anything.

Dad also looked rather shocked as Georgina and I came through the door, but I gave him a look that said, "I'll tell you later." He kindly pretended not to notice the missing shoe, but raised his eyebrows at me when I turned to look back at him from the stairs. Georgina was hobbling up in front of me, every step she took crashing on the boards. Mom, I supposed, must have been totally lost in the wilds of Storyland not to have heard the racket.

I managed to find some old shoes that were about Georgina's size. She glanced around my room. "Not too bad, I suppose," she said grudgingly.

I hadn't really thought about it before, but I guess the room did look pretty cozy now. Our great-great aunt's furniture, together with all my odds and ends, made it inviting and comfortable. There was a big old-fashioned chest of drawers that doubled as a dressing table. On it stood an oval mirror with a wooden base.

"Cool," said Georgina quietly, adjusting the mirror so she could see her reflection. "I don't have anything like this at home."

"It belonged to the old lady who owned the place," I said, "just like the..."

Then a new idea struck me.

"Like the house," I finished hastily. "Won't your mother be wondering where you are, too?"

Georgina sighed quietly. "I suppose so. I'd better go."

I saw her out the front door, then went back to my room to think. Cilla had made a cat-nest on my bed, and she was purring herself to sleep.

I idly swung the mirror back and forth. I'd never really looked at it closely before, especially the carved pattern decorating the bottom part. I ran my fingers over it and, to my surprise, discovered that part of the base lifted up!

Inside was a photograph. It was posed, like a publicity shot. A woman wearing a top hat and tails was sitting on a wooden chair, a tuba on her knees. "Good luck, Irene" was scrawled across it.

As I stared at the photo I suddenly remembered the poster at the shop. There was some connection, I was sure. I had to go back and take a closer look.

FIVE

The Tuba Players

I opened the green-painted door of the store. I'd left Cilla behind this time, just in case!

Alice's head popped up from behind the counter, like a rabbit out of its burrow.

"Come in, come in!" she cried. "Nice to see you again so soon."

"Er – it's nice to see you, too. I was just wondering if I could have another look at that poster I found yesterday."

The caretaker's dandelion head appeared out of the dimness at the back of the store. "Of course you can," he smiled, "if you can find it!"

I looked, dismayed, at the shelves piled with posters, newspaper clippings, and old magazines.

Alice turned on a lamp with a pink fluted shade like a flower. "It's all right, dear – I was looking at it again after you left. I know exactly the one you mean. It was one of the Sisters. I'll go and get it."

"What does she mean – the Sisters?" I asked the caretaker.

"The Sisters of Swing. They were very popular. They used to play next door a lot."

"An all-woman band?"

Alice giggled as she came back into the room with the rolled-up poster and a big ragged book. She sounded much younger than she looked. "You could hardly have men in a band called The Sisters of Swing! They played for dances, or in theaters like the one next door."

The caretaker smiled at his sister. "She's being modest. Alice *was* one of the Sisters. Played the trumpet!"

Alice gave me the poster and opened the old scrapbook. As she turned the pages, I started to recognize the names of the towns. Then I remembered – they were the same as the ones on the old trunk at home!

Excitedly, I unrolled the poster. Surely the one at the back, on the left-hand side, was...

"Alice, who was your tuba player?"

"Why, Irene Florimell was her name. She was a terrific player. Got married, left the band."

And their white bow-ties...The last piece of the puzzle fell into place. "SS" stood for "The Sisters of Swing." Alice and my great-great-aunt had played together in the band!

When I told Alice and her brother they were delighted. "Let's have a toast!" cried Alice, as she went away to find some juice.

I went back to the store often, to hear all about the Sisters. And I took Irene's things and the photo to show Alice and her brother. My great-great-aunt – what a woman! It gave me a good feeling to be linked with her – a good strong branch on our family tree.

And as for me – I really like school now. I owned up about the invented family tree, and took Irene's hat, tie and tails and the poster and photo along to show everyone. And I arranged for Alice to visit with her scrapbook and talk to the class about the famous Sisters! Ms. Parkinson was even more impressed now. Georgina couldn't say anything this time, because she knew I was telling the truth. And Amanda and Jacinta liked Irene's story so much that they wanted to be friends with me.

In fact, we've decided to form our own band – and I'm learning to play the tuba! Georgina's going to be the drummer. We're

still thinking about which instruments would be best for Amanda and Jacinta.

Alice is full of helpful hints, and Cilla has been recruited as our mascot. Tom wants to be our manager, but I'm not quite sure if The New Sisters of Swing are really ready for that yet – and anyway, I think we can probably take care of ourselves!

TITLES IN THE SERIES